A Whispering Coyote Book
First published in the United States of America in 2001 by
Charlesbridge Publishing
85 Main Street
Watertown, MA 02472
(617) 926-0329
www.charlesbridge.com

Library of Congress Cataloging-in-Publication data is available upon request.

Printed in Belgium
(hc) 10 9 8 7 6 5 4 3 2 1

Sidney Won't SWIM

Hilde Schuurmans

Whispering Coyote
A Charlesbridge Imprint

"See you tomorrow, class," said Miss Lisa.
"Don't forget to bring your swimsuits. Tomorrow
is your first swimming lesson!"

"Ugh," Sidney muttered. "Swimming is dumb."

Mom was waiting for him at the school gate.
"Hi, Sidney! What's wrong? You look upset."

"Tomorrow is our first swimming lesson,"
Sidney complained.

"Oh, how nice," Mom replied.

"Nice? Swimming isn't nice," Sidney said
angrily. "Swimming is the dumbest thing in
the whole world!"

"You're just saying that because it's
your first time," Mom reassured him.
"Are you a tiny bit scared of the water?"

"I'm not scared," Sidney grumped.
"I just think swimming is dumb."

Sidney was still so upset at dinner that night that he couldn't eat a thing. "There's no need to be afraid, Sidney," Dad tried to comfort him. "Swimming isn't that hard."

"I'm not afraid!" Sidney yelled. "Swimming is dumb, that's all. I don't want to swim." Sidney was really mad now. He stomped off to his room and wouldn't come out for dessert.

At bedtime Mom tucked him in, but Sidney couldn't sleep. He thought and thought, and he muttered and moped, and then he thought some more. The whole time he could think of only one thing: swimming.

"I'm not afraid," Sidney told himself firmly. "Swimming is boring. Swimming is silly. Swimming is wet and dull and . . . swimming is . . . dumb, and . . . I'm not afraid . . . swim . . . is . . . zzzz. . . ."

"Good morning, Sidney, time to get up!" Mom called.

"I don't feel good," Sidney groaned. "My tummy aches, and I have a fever. I can't go swimming today."

"My poor Sidney—I'll get the thermometer. Hmm . . . ," said Mom after she had taken his temperature. She winked at Dad. "You're right, Sidney. This doesn't look very good at all. You can't possibly go swimming today. We'd better go see the doctor instead."

"The doctor?" Sidney asked in alarm. "Oh no! I feel much better now. I don't have a tummy ache anymore," and he quickly hopped out of bed.

"OK, if you're sure," Mom said with a smile. "Come on, we have to hurry. You don't want to be late for school."

The morning passed quickly in class, and soon Miss Lisa announced that it was time to get on the bus and go to the pool. All the other kids rushed out to get the best seats, but Sidney lagged behind.

"What's wrong, Sidney?" asked Miss Lisa.

"I left my swimming bag in the classroom," Sidney answered.

"Go and get it as quickly as you can, then. We have to go," Miss Lisa insisted.

Sidney turned and ran as fast as he could. When he got to the other side of the schoolyard wall, he dropped down to hide behind it. "No one will find me here," he thought.

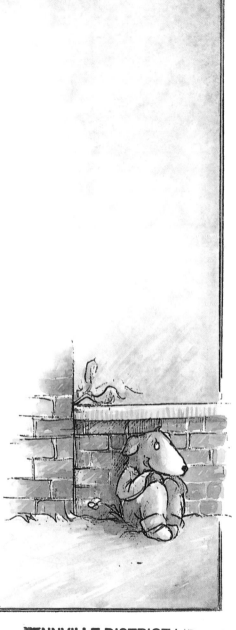

"What are you doing, Sidney?" It was Miss Lisa!

"Um . . . I'm still looking for my swimming bag," Sidney fibbed.

"Tell me, Sidney," Miss Lisa said, "are you a little afraid to go swimming?"

"No way!" Sidney cried angrily. "It's just that . . . swimming is dumb."

"How do you know unless you try it?" Miss Lisa coaxed.

Sidney frowned. He didn't want to try it. Not ever! But Miss Lisa kept standing there, so he had to get his swimming bag and climb onto the bus.

In the locker room, most of the other kids seemed excited about learning how to swim. But to Sidney, some of them also looked a bit nervous.

"I'm not afraid," thought Sidney. "I just don't want to swim, that's all. Swimming is dumb and boring." He decided to hide in one of the changing rooms and lock the door. He hoped nobody would notice that he was gone.

"Sidney? Are you in here?" It was Miss Lisa again.

"I'm here. . . ," Sidney mumbled.

"Are you ready for your swimming lesson?" Miss Lisa asked.

Sidney heaved a great big sigh. "Yes, I'm ready." Together, Sidney and Miss Lisa walked toward the swimming pool.

"Hi, you must be Sidney. My name is Paul, and I'm the swimming teacher. Are you ready to go in the water?"

"No!" Sidney shouted.

"No? Why not?" Mr. Paul asked patiently.

"Well . . . when I get wet, I turn into a huge monster!" Sidney told him.

"A monster? That's terrible! I guess you'd better not swim, after all. Imagine that—a monster!" Mr. Paul marveled. "Maybe you could watch what the other kids do, instead," he suggested.

"All right," Sidney agreed. He felt relieved.

Sidney sat at the edge of the pool, watching his classmates splash around. While Mr. Paul explained about different swimming strokes, Sidney's friends Sam and Lucy giggled behind his back.

"Hee, hee, hee," Sam laughed. "How silly. Turning into a monster when you get in the water—I'd sure like to see that." Suddenly he pushed Sidney into the pool!

"Run for your lives! A monster! A monster!" Lucy shouted. She and Sam ran away, laughing and screaming and pretending to be terrified.

Sidney sank straight to the bottom, but Mr. Paul quickly grabbed his arms and lifted him out of the water. Sidney coughed and choked and started to cry. "I'm afraid of the water," he sobbed. "I don't want to swim!"

Mr. Paul was very angry with Sam and Lucy. "That wasn't very nice of you, and it wasn't very smart," he scolded. "Sidney might have drowned." Sam and Lucy felt terrible.

"I was kind of scared the first time I went in the pool," Sam admitted sheepishly.

"Once you know what it feels like, it isn't so bad," added Lucy.

"Really?" Sidney asked, and he tried to stop crying.

"We'll help you," his friends promised.

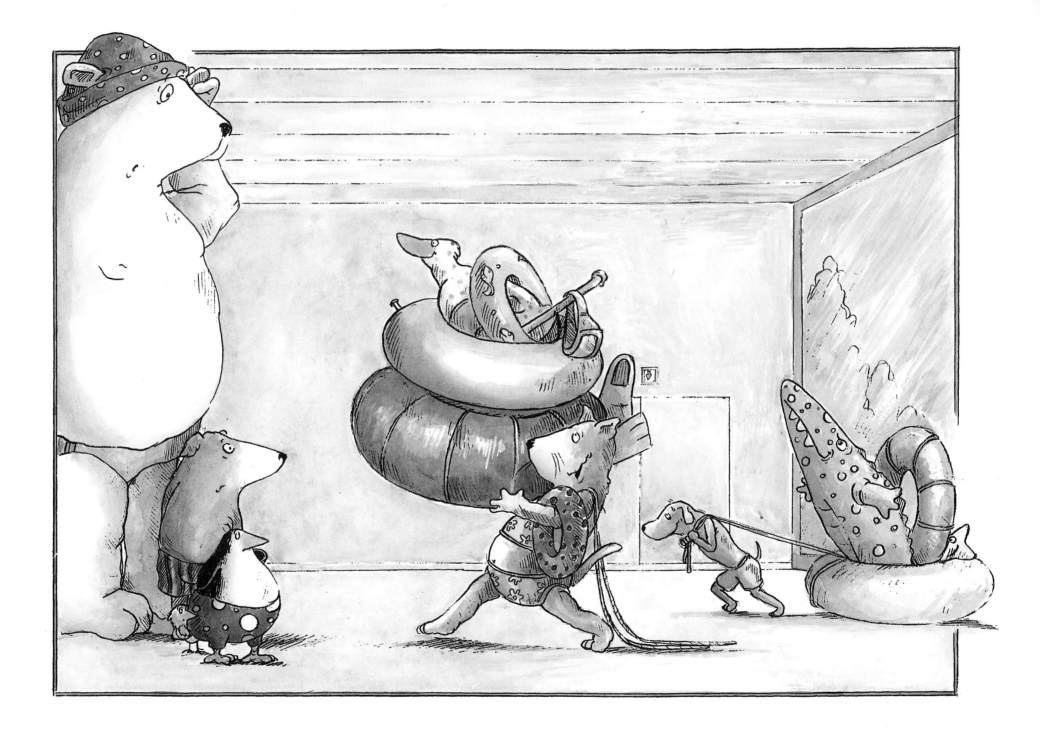

Sam and Lucy walked all the way around the pool, picking up as much swimming equipment as they could find. They gathered flippers, a diving mask, six inflatable tubes, and lots of other toys. Then they set to work inventing something that would stop Sidney from drowning. They tried this way, then that way, but nothing seemed quite right. Finally, they came up with the perfect solution.

"Ta-dah!"

A big Sidney-monster drifted across the water
while the rest of the class cheered and clapped.

"Swimming isn't dumb," Sidney shouted
happily. "Swimming is fun!"